A HUMAN AT THE HOTEL

HOTEL TRANSYLVANIA
THE SERIES

A HUMAN AT THE HOTEL

Adapted by Cala Spinner

Simon Spotlight
New York London Toronto Sydney New Delhi

SIMON SPOTLIGHT

An imprint of Simon & Schuster Children's Publishing Division

1230 Avenue of the Americas, New York, New York 10020

This Simon Spotlight edition August 2018

TM & © 2018 Sony Pictures Animation Inc. All Rights Reserved.

All rights reserved, including the right of reproduction in whole or in part in any form.

SIMON SPOTLIGHT and colophon are registered trademarks of Simon & Schuster, Inc.

For information about special discounts for bulk purchases, please contact Simon & Schuster Special Sales at 1-866-506-1949 or business@simonandschuster.com.

Designed by Bob Steimle

Manufactured in the United States of America 0718 LAK

10 9 8 7 6 5 4 3 2 1

ISBN 978-1-5344-2707-5 (hc)

ISBN 978-1-5344-2706-8 (pbk)

ISBN 978-1-5344-2708-2 (eBook)

CHAPTER ONE

Mavis Dracula wasn't an average teenager—she was a *vampire* teenager. That meant she could do lots of supercool things, like turn into a bat and fly through the air. But being a vampire wasn't all fun and games. Mavis wasn't allowed to go out into the human world, and could only hang out with other monsters. That was because her father, Drac, thought humans wanted to destroy all of monsterkind. He had built the Hotel Transylvania—a hotel just for monsters— to keep Mavis safe. Since it opened, no human had ever been inside.

There was no safer place for a monster to be. But Mavis wanted freedom. One day, when her father had to leave the hotel to meet with the Vampire Council, Mavis thought she would finally have the chance to be in charge of the hotel.

She was wrong. Drac called upon his sister, Lydia, the Dark Baroness, to watch over Mavis and the Hotel Transylvania. Unfortunately, Aunt Lydia was even *more* strict than Drac . . . and *scarier* too!

Mavis had just rescued her friend Wendy the Blob from being stuck inside a ketchup bottle when she heard some interesting news.

It came from a decorative shrunken head that hung on a doorknob in the hallway. "Hey, Mavis!" the shrunken head said when she walked by. "Did you hear? Gretchen Squib from *Scream-Cation* is coming to review the hotel today!"

Mavis gasped.

"Today?" she said.

Mavis couldn't believe it. *Scream-Cation* was a very important travel newspaper for monsters—and Gretchen Squib was a tough critic!

"One bad review and she can sink the hotel!" Mavis said. "Aunt Lydia demanded that I 'maintain order' so nothing goes wrong. Which really just means, 'Do nothing,'" Mavis said, pouting.

"But . . . you're not going to do that?" Wendy guessed.

Mavis began to pace back and forth . . . first on the floor, and then on the ceiling! She desperately wanted to prove she could do more than her dad or her aunt expected of her, so she quickly hatched a plan. "I'll fix up the hotel myself, nail the review, land us a five-skull rating, *and* score all the credit!"

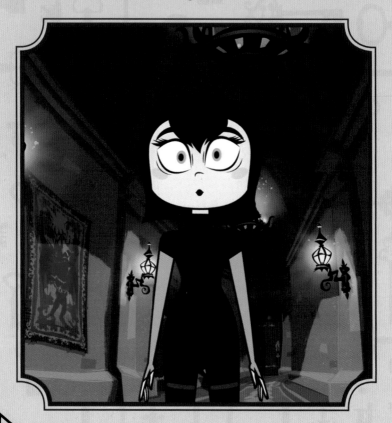

Mavis got right to work on her hotel improvement project to get everything ready for Gretchen's arrival. She spotted a nearby door that was nailed shut with unsightly pieces of wood, and started to pry them off the doorframe.

"Not that I don't *totally* believe you, Mavis, because I do, but this sounds like the kind of thing that always blows up right in your face," said Wendy, watching as Mavis struggled to pull off the last piece of wood.

"Oh, come on. How's this going to blow—" Mavis started to say, but before she could finish, the door flew open and she was almost trampled by a pack of werewolf pups that came running out of the room!

The wolf pups barreled down the hallway and ran into a nearby zombie bellhop pulling a pile of suitcases on a wooden cart. The suitcases flew

in the air . . . and when they landed, the zombie's uniform had been replaced with a hotel guest's pink bathing suit and pearl necklace!

"Huh?" the zombie bellhop moaned, confused.

Mavis didn't have time to laugh at his new clothing. She raced after the wolf pups, hoping to catch them before Aunt Lydia did.

Another shrunken head decoration felt the need to comment on Mavis's plan when she ran by its door. "Totally going to blow up in her face," it said matter-of-factly.

But Mavis was already gone!

CHAPTER TWO

The wolf pups had taken hold of the rope attached to the zombie's luggage cart and were pulling it through the hotel like a dogsled. Mavis ran as fast as she could until she finally got close enough to hop onto the cart, but that didn't mean she had control of the pups. They just pulled her with them!

Going for the ride, Mavis suddenly realized that one of the wolf pups was missing!

"Wait a sec. Where's Winnie?" she wondered aloud.

If Winnie wasn't with the rest of her pack . . . it meant she was roaming free around the hotel!

Unfortunately, Mavis didn't have much time to come up with a plan. The wolf pups dragged her into the hotel lobby, which was the worst place to go . . . because Aunt Lydia was there.

Aunt Lydia was admiring a new statue—of herself—that she was having installed in the main area of the hotel. As zombies carefully carried the statue down the stairs and past the reception desk, the wolf pups slammed into a mariachi band and a

housekeeping witch. Before Mavis could stop the pups, they rammed into the statue of Aunt Lydia and broke it completely in half.

It was the worst possible scenario.

"Rah!" Aunt Lydia roared and tapped her magical staff. She then used a freezing spell to make everyone freeze in midair—everyone except for Mavis, who fell off the cart and tumbled down the stairs, landing at Aunt Lydia's feet.

"Ahem." Aunt Lydia cleared her throat.

"Aunt Lydia!" Mavis called, pretending to be surprised. "Hi! I was just . . . getting us ready for the review! You know, with my dad away at the Vampire

Council, I'm, like, basically in charge."

"Except you're not in charge," Aunt Lydia said with her fangs bared. "*I* am."

Aunt Lydia towered over Mavis, looking even scarier than usual, so Mavis tried to lighten the mood.

"That's why I said, 'like, basically,'" she reasoned, and tiptoed over to Wendy, who was still frozen in midair. "Anyway, I'm 'maintaining order.' Look! I found all but one wolf pup, and when you think about how many there are, that's really pretty good."

Mavis was a quick thinker, but Aunt Lydia wasn't buying it.

"Young lady, Hotel Transylvania has had a sterling reputation for a thousand years. Loose wolf pups upset order. Secrets upset order. *Teenage vampires* upset order," Aunt Lydia said. With each thing that "upset order," fire erupted from Aunt Lydia's staff to help her make her point.

Mavis raised her hand. "Just a quick question," she said, and tapped on a frozen zombie bellhop nearby. "Doesn't freezing people upset order?"

"You will maintain order or it is puppy duty for you," Aunt Lydia said, pretending she hadn't heard Mavis's question.

Mavis gulped. The "puppy" that Aunt Lydia was referring to wasn't a puppy at all—it was the three-headed monster dog, Cerberus, who lived in a pit under the hotel. Mavis was terrified of Cerberus—and she wasn't someone who was easily scared.

"Uh, great," Mavis said. "Just so I'm clear, finding the lost wolf pup would count as a first step in maintaining order?"

Aunt Lydia didn't bother to answer. She was done with the conversation. She tapped her staff twice, even though her pet chicken, Diane, was on top of it. Then she disappeared in a puff of purple smoke and flames.

When Aunt Lydia was gone, everyone who had been frozen in midair toppled to the ground.

"I'll take that as a yes," Mavis groaned.

Now she had to find Winnie the wolf pup—before Gretchen Squib or Aunt Lydia found her first.

CHAPTER THREE

Thankfully, Mavis had an idea of where to look. First, she grabbed a dessert cart from the hotel kitchen. Then she pushed it through the grounds of Hotel Transylvania, trailed by her friends Wendy, Hank N Stein, and Pedro. While they walked, Mavis dropped pieces of cake on the ground behind them.

"So, remind me again. Why are you wasting perfectly good cake?" Hank asked.

"I'm not wasting it, Hank," Mavis was quick to respond. "I'm using it! I don't have time to hunt for the wolf pup, so I'm bringing the wolf pup to me."

"With *ground* cake?" Wendy asked.

"Devil's Food Cake, to be precise," Mavis said, holding up a slice.

As if on cue, the cake took on the appearance of a devil! Its frosting turned into a pair of horns and two beady eyes, and its layers became a devilish mouth.

Then, to prove her point, the cake slice spoke. "I'm *delicious*," it growled in a surprisingly low voice.

"What *he* said," Mavis quipped.

"Know who else loves cake?" Pedro said, looking through a pair of binoculars he had brought along.

"Who?" asked Mavis, innocently.

"Humans," Pedro said as he pointed out a little red-haired human girl riding in a toy car just outside the hotel's gates.

"Oh no!" Mavis gasped. Her cake trap had worked—but instead of attracting Winnie the wolf

pup, she'd lured a human to the hotel instead!

"You've caught the Nose Picker, from that human tribe across the way!" said Pedro, calling the toddler by the nickname they had given it because they sometimes spotted it picking its nose.

"The Nose Picker," Wendy repeated. "You know, I always thought she was just a myth, like sweet potatoes, or unicorns," she said, ignoring the fact that

Hank was chattering with fear at the mere thought of a human.

Mavis guessed that the baby lived in a house built on a cliff across from Hotel Transylvania, and her parents were probably worried. Mavis hoped the little girl would steer her toy car back to her family, but instead, she watched in horror as the girl drove closer and closer to the hotel.

"Holy rabies," Mavis said when the little girl drove over the bridge and through the arched gate surrounding Hotel Transylvania. "She went into the hotel! Aunt Lydia will freak!" And then Mavis noticed something even *worse*—Winnie was

following the baby! "We've got to find the human before Aunt Lydia does or she'll never believe I can run things," Mavis said. Then she darted away, desperate to fix it.

On a nearby winding road, Gretchen Squib was driving her bright yellow car to Hotel Transylvania.

Inside the hotel, it was clear that time was running out for everyone to put things in order.

"Five minutes till Gretchen is here," announced a shrunken head.

Meanwhile, Aunt Lydia had other concerns. She sniffed the air at the bottom of the staircase, and her face lit up.

"I smell human," Aunt Lydia realized. "It has been *centuries* since I've been on a good human hunt."

Aunt Lydia's pet chicken, Diane, was perched on

the top of her staff. "Centuries!" Diane mimicked Aunt Lydia. Then she made a clucking noise, fell off the staff, and tumbled to the ground. Aunt Lydia didn't even seem to notice.

"If there is a human in this hotel, I will find it. And I will *eat* it!" Aunt Lydia vowed, suddenly looking a bit like a devil.

Poor Diane had stood up, but she got so scared that she laid an egg . . . and then fell on it. The egg cracked and splattered all over the floor!

Aunt Lydia chuckled. She had been joking, but it didn't seem very funny to Diane.

"Well, I likely won't eat it, but a scolding it will get!" Aunt Lydia said, wiping her eyes as she laughed. Then she glided away as a witch came to clean up the eggy mess.

CHAPTER FOUR

Mavis scoured the hallways, searching for the Nose Picker and Winnie the wolf pup. Suddenly she heard barking. Winnie was riding in the toy car alongside the Nose Picker!

Mavis smiled wide. "Nose Picker *and* Winnie! It's a two-for-one!" she said, and transformed into a bat and began flying as fast as she could to catch up with them.

Mavis reached them right as the Nose Picker drove into a wall and bounced out of the car. Mavis transformed backed into her human self and snatched the kid before anyone got hurt.

"Gotcha!" she called, hugging the Nose Picker close and spinning her around. Meanwhile, Winnie toppled into Pedro, who was exhausted from running so fast.

It seemed like things were going well . . . until Mavis heard a spooky voice.

"Where is that human?"

It was Aunt Lydia's spooky voice!

"Shh! We've got to hide you!" Mavis told the Nose Picker. She stuffed the Nose Picker and Pedro into a chute in the wall and stowed Winnie and the toy car away in a housekeeping cart that was covered with a piece of cloth. Mavis heard Aunt Lydia get closer and hoped her plan would work.

Moments later, Aunt Lydia arrived at the spot. But instead of the Nose Picker, she found only Mavis.

"Mavis! What are you hiding?" Aunt Lydia called.

Mavis paused for a second, then threw open her arms.

"Fine," Mavis said, faking a lighthearted laugh. Then she reached into the housekeeping cart and pulled out the toy car . . . with Winnie the wolf pup in the driver's seat. "Good thing I caught her so she couldn't upset the order of the hotel, huh?" Mavis said, pointing at the wolf pup.

Aunt Lydia's eyes narrowed.

"And I guess *this*," Mavis continued, holding up the toy car, "explains the human smell. Order *maintained*," she said, then brushed her hands together to show that the case was closed.

Aunt Lydia roared. She had really wanted to go on a human hunt . . . but she quickly decided to accept the situation for what it was. She motioned toward the toy car. "Very well. We shall incinerate the car before any of the guests catch the *disgusting* human scent."

"Pretty car!" Diane clucked. She wanted to drive it even though she was a chicken!

Aunt Lydia sighed. "Ugh, fine," she told Diane, who promptly hopped into the car and grabbed the wheel with a wing. "Well, I guess if it makes you feel like a chick again."

In a flash Diane sped through the halls, clucking and chirping, with Aunt Lydia gliding eerily behind her.

Then a real-life car pulled up to Hotel Transylvania. It was Gretchen Squib's.

"She's here!" wailed one of the shrunken heads.

"Oh no," Mavis mumbled. The Nose Picker and Pedro were still hidden in the chute in the wall! What if Gretchen saw them during her inspection?

Mavis peered inside the chute, but no one was there. Hank and Wendy looked too, but all they could see was an empty tube headed to the bottom of the hotel.

"Where do you think that goes?" Wendy asked.

Mavis suddenly knew the answer, and unfortunately it hadn't occurred to her when she hid the Nose Picker and Pedro in the chute. There was only one place the chute could lead *all the way down* to: the pit deep below the hotel . . . where Cerberus the three-headed dog lived!

CHAPTER FIVE

Mavis, Winnie, Wendy, and Hank burst through the door to Cerberus's pit. Sure enough, Pedro and the Nose Picker were there, and so was Cerberus. It was as large as a house, with three snarling dog heads and three sets of sharp teeth . . . but it didn't seem to be bothering anyone.

Even so, Pedro was terrified of it. He had his eyes closed and was standing off to the side, repeatedly telling himself to "go to your happy place, go to your happy place!" Try as he might, though, Pedro was still in the pit with Cerberus, and he wasn't happy.

The Nose Picker, on the other hand, seemed to be having a great time. She was jumping up and down on Cerberus's giant belly!

Mavis shut the pit door as fast as she could. "Order . . . not . . . maintained!" she huffed, holding the door closed. She needed a find a way to get to Pedro and the Nose Picker without upsetting Cerberus. "Okay, Mavis, *think*. There's gotta be something worse than a three-headed dog." Just then, Winnie bit Mavis's ankle, which gave her an idea: Wild werewolf pups could be really scary! If she could get the pups to come to the pit, she could scare Cerberus and buy time to stage a rescue. "Hank! Didn't you take three years of wolf pup calling?" she asked.

Hank cleared his throat.

"*Four* years, actually," he corrected her, holding up four fingers.

But Mavis didn't care for Hank's bragging. "Can you just do it, please?" she demanded.

"Okay," Hank said. He stood up straight, stuck his tongue out as far as it would go, and made it ripple as he yelled . . . but didn't appear to be making a sound.

Mavis crossed her arms.

"I'm guessing that didn't work," Wendy observed.

A second later, the wolf pups ran toward Mavis and her friends.

Mavis knew what she had to do. She opened the door to Cerberus's pit. The wolf pups ran in, and Cerberus was terrified! He climbed up the chain hanging from the roof of the pit, trying to escape the little pups on the ground.

The chaos gave Mavis time to grab the Nose Picker. She held the human in her arms and smiled. "See? No problem," Mavis said.

At this, Pedro perked up. He smiled now too.

"You all know I was faking, right?" he declared, but no one believed him.

Mavis brought the Nose Picker over to the pack

of wolf pups and gave them instructions. "All right, I need you guys to get her home before anybody finds out," she said.

The wolf pups saluted and then formed a tight pack so the Nose Picker could sit on their backs as they ran. They darted out of the pit . . . and headed straight to the lobby!

"No, not through the lobby! Stop!" Mavis cried as she and her friends chased after them.

CHAPTER SIX

In the lobby, the zombie bellhops were in the process of bringing out the statue of Aunt Lydia, which they had tried to repair with green tape that covered it from head to toe. Aunt Lydia was supervising the process.

"Careful with my *beautiful* statue," Aunt Lydia instructed a zombie.

But before he could respond, the wolf pups and the Nose Picker raced in! They knocked into the bellhop and broke Aunt Lydia's statue, *again*. The statue's head flew off and landed on the real Aunt

Lydia's head, and then she caught one of its stone arms in each of her hands and frowned.

The wolf pups just kept running! They zoomed past Bigfoot, who was by the hotel's revolving doors, ran outside the gates, and headed toward the little house where the Nose Picker lived to return the human to her people.

Inside the hotel, Bigfoot had tried to stomp on the wolf pups . . . but ended up smashing the furniture instead. Then he accidentally sat down right on the roaring fire in the lobby's fireplace! Bigfoot hopped up again—he wasn't hurt—but Hank freaked out.

"Fire! Fire, fire, fire!" Hank screamed. He was so afraid that he ran straight through a wall, making a big hole in it. Then a chandelier came tumbling to the ground. Everything was falling apart!

Pedro emerged from Cerberus's pit and gasped. "Whoa," he said.

The entire hotel was in shambles, but there was no time to fix it.

"Announcing Gretchen Squib," said one of the shrunken heads.

A short little monster with purple wings and curly orange hair flew in, frowning.

"What's going on here?" Gretchen asked.

Smoke spilled out from the fireplace. Furniture was on its side. A housekeeping witch bumbled through the scene, mopping whatever she could. It

was the worst possible way for a reviewer to see the hotel!

"No!" Aunt Lydia wailed.

Mavis braced herself for bad news and covered her eyes.

Gretchen Squib held out a clipboard and pen,

ready to write everything up. To everyone's surprise, Gretchen's frown turned to a giant smile, and her eyes lit up.

"I . . . love it!" Gretchen said, talking about the hotel.

"Huh?" Mavis mumbled, bringing her hands down from her eyes.

Gretchen Squib loved the mess! She gave Hotel Transylvania a five-skull rating in the *Scream-Cation* newspaper. Boom-drac-a-lacka!

There was one thing that Gretchen didn't like, though. She flew over to Aunt Lydia and glared at the statue head sitting atop her head.

"Ew," Gretchen said, and docked a half-skull from her rating, leaving them with four and a half skulls.

Then, without a word, Gretchen left to review the next hotel on her list. When she was gone, Mavis smiled at Aunt Lydia.

"Could be worse," Mavis said cautiously.

"Could it?" asked Aunt Lydia, scowling. She stood motionless, but the statue head that had fallen on top of her own head suddenly fell to the ground and split in half.

58

It had been a crazy day, but Mavis was happy. Whatever Aunt Lydia thought, the hotel had received a great rating! As long as he didn't find out about the human visitor to the hotel, Mavis figured Drac would be quite proud!